The Anti-Muffins
by
Madeleine L'Engle

The Anti-Muffins
by
Madeleine L'Engle

Illustrated by
Gloria Ortíz

The Pilgrim Press
New York, Philadelphia

The Pilgrim Press, 132 W. 31 Street, New York, New York 10001

Library of Congress Cataloging in Publication Data
L'Engle, Madeleine.
   The anti-muffins.
   (The Education of the public and the public school)
   I. Title.   II. Series: Education of the public and the public school.
PS3523.E55A83   813'.54   80-21425
ISBN 0-8298-0415-3

Introduction

"Education in the schools as well as education in the home, church and community is under critical examination. To meet the urgent needs of all persons, especially those of children and youth, the church is called to the renewal of a long standing commitment to secure for each child of God that education which will fully develop his or her capacities and which will enable that person to serve as a responsible person in the common life. This commitment is based on our belief that there are coherent patterns of purpose and meaning in human life to which education must point if it is to assist humankind in the pursuit of truth and the fulfillment of human destiny. Participation in efforts to improve education is a continuing moral responsibility for every Christian." (From "The Church and the Public School," a position paper of the United Church Board for Homeland Ministries, May, 1979)

The public school is not lacking for doomsayers or critics; they are as abundant as the locusts and frogs of the plagues of Egypt. Nor is the public school lacking in moral cheerleaders who have their own righteous demands of what the school is to be and to do; they are as abundant as the tongues of Babel. There is no abundance, however, of persons and groups who perceive what is at stake for all of the people of the republic and for the republic itself in the present crisis in the public school and who accept their public responsibility for the welfare of the public school.

The monograph series is issued not as a directive from the church to the public school but as an aid to persons in the churches and the public at large who care about the public school and who, with others in their communities, seek a basis for understanding and addressing some of the complex problems of their public schools.

The monographs are published by the United Church Board for Homeland Ministries whose own tradition of commitment to the education of the public reaches back to the settlement of the nation and whose tradition of commitment to the public school extends to its formation in seventeenth century New England. This tradition respects and advocates the distinctiveness of the role of the church and the school but it also recognizes their common responsibility for the welfare of

5

persons and the society. We hope these monographs strengthen that common commitment.

Members of the Public Education Issue Group which developed the monographs include Percel O. Alston, Robert A. Mayo, Audrey Miller and Verlyn Barker, Chairperson, from the staff of United Church Board for Homeland Ministries, and Harold Viehman, staff, United Ministries in Education. Douglas Sloan, Professor of History and Education and Editor of the *Teachers College Record*, Teachers College, Columbia University, served as an invaluable Consultant to the Issue Group.

Verlyn L. Barker

The Education of the Public and the Public School

A Monograph Series of the
UNITED CHURCH BOARD FOR HOMELAND MINISTRIES

Howard E. Spragg, Executive Vice-President

Verlyn L. Barker, Editor
Audrey Miller, Managing Editor
Douglas Sloan, Consulting Editor

Every once in a while something happens to make you realize you don't know someone you thought you knew inside out. My brother, John, for instance. John is older than I am, so I've known him all my life, and Suzy and Rob most of my life, since they're younger. John's always been my big brother, and I've admired him and loved him and hated him and fought with him and never thought much about him simply because he's just John.

And our father. Daddy's a country doctor, and he's in and out at all times of day and night, and he's comfortable and to be climbed on and rough-housed with when we're small, and then lap sat and cuddled, and then just given a hug and kiss at bed-time as we get older. But he's familiar, and it's hard for us to realize that lots of people are afraid of him.

And Mother. She's just mother to us, and yet there are people to whom she is first and foremost Victoria Eaton Austin, that clever entertainer, and quite different from the person we know and love.

So of course the John we see isn't the John anybody else sees, and that's a big thing to realize.

It all started out with measles. All in one week John and Maggy and Suzy and Rob all came down with measles, in chronological order. Maggy is living with us for the time being, because she's an orphan, and her grandfather is old and ill and lives alone in a mansion in New York. Having Maggy as part of the family hasn't been easy, because she was spoiled rotten and thought she was the center of the universe, and then the universe betrayed her by letting her

parents die; we've had to remind ourselves
frequently that she has good reason for being
difficult.

Anyhow, the other kids all got measles and I
didn't, heaven knows why. So I helped Mother
take care of the others because she said there
wasn't any point in trying to isolate me; I was
already thoroughly exposed and I might as well
make myself useful. This mostly meant taking
care of Rob, who's only five. Maggy's two years
younger than I am, twelve, and Suzy a year
younger than Maggy, eleven.

Everybody was miserable, everybody had
high fevers, but Rob was the most miserable of
all. His head ached and his eyes hurt and every
part of him was uncomfortable, and any time Rob
is hurt or sick he believes in letting everybody
know about it. So this time he thought he was
much sicker than the others, and Daddy said he
was, a little, but not nearly as much as he thought
he was.

John lay in the guest room with Rochester,
our Great Dane, by his bed, when Rochester could
be called away from Rob. Mother put up the dart
board on the wall across from his bed and he
threw darts. And then he played records. He
played Mother's records, and his album of country
and western, and Mother said if she heard *The
Gambler* one more time she'd break the record
over his head, measles or no. He wanted to watch
television, but the TV is downstairs and Daddy
said it wasn't good for his eyes, which are a bit
weak, anyhow. We seem to watch a lot less
television than most of our friends, partly because
our parents limit our watching, but largely
because there's so much else to do.

Daddy brought home two small dolls for
Maggy and Suzy and they lay in bed and played
with the dolls and slept and complained. Suzy
pretended both the dolls had smallpox and she
was a famous doctor taking care of them during
an outbreak of smallpox because, she said, people
got careless about vaccinations. And she had
Maggy's doll die of smallpox, and then Maggy
shrieked and yelled and screamed herself to a
pulp, and Mother said Suzy would have to invent
a new serum to resurrect Maggy's doll, and Suzy
felt mean because she was sick, and she said the
doll was dead and she was going to perform an
autopsy, and Maggy leaped out of bed and
grabbed Suzy's doll and pulled off one of its arms
and they started to have a free-for-all, and Mother
had to send Suzy into her bed to wait until Daddy
came home.

And Rob just felt miserable. Mother was so busy with the others that I stayed with Rob. I drew the curtains at the windows and got my big soft quilt and rocked him and sang to him and told him stories, and Colette, our little grey dog, cuddled with us, too, and I discovered again how terribly much I love my bratty little brother.

So everybody got over measles and went back to school. The incubation period went by, and Daddy said, "Well, Vicky, it looks as though you have a natural immunity to measles."

But the next day in school my head began to ache, and my eyeballs began to throb, and if you've never had measles you haven't any idea how awful you feel. So about eleven o'clock my teacher called Mother, and she and Rob got in the station wagon and came over and brought me home. Mother said, "Well, Vicky, it looks as though you weren't immune to measles after all, but you certainly waited till beyond the last minute to get them."

I undressed and Mother turned down my bed and when I got in the sheets felt cool, and the pillow soft and good to my head. Rob brought me up a glass of gingerale, and that tasted just perfect, and I felt quite cozy and contented. But then my head began throbbing and my eyeballs hurting and the pillow was hot and the bed had lumps and the sheets instead of feeling smooth were suddenly scratchy, and I realized how good Rob had been while he was so miserable. And I was lucky because I was the only one who was sick, so Mother could pay more attention to me. She sat by the bed and stroked my head with cool fingers, and Rochester flopped down by the bed as much as to say he'd take care of me, too. When the others got back from school they came in and said they were sorry, because they knew how miserable I felt, and Suzy fixed my bed, straightened the sheets and turned the pillow so it felt cool again. When John got home from the Regional High School he said I could have the dart board; he'd put it up for me; but I didn't feel like throwing darts. I didn't feel like watching television. I didn't even feel like listening to Mother's records, so I knew I was really sick.

Rob went into the guest room with John that night so I wouldn't disturb him with my tossing and turning and my feverish bouncings, and so he wouldn't disturb me if he snored. But I was used to having Rob's small bed at the foot of my big pine bedstead. I didn't want him to go. I cried and that made my eyes worse. John came in to say good-night and to bring me aspirin, and said, "I guess I was just lucky and didn't have it as bad as you, Vic. Even with my myopic eyes my head didn't ache much after the first day. Maybe you'll feel like playing darts or something tomorrow. I don't suppose you'd like me to set up my electric train in here where you can see it?"

John's electric train used to belong to our Uncle Douglas, and it's got all kinds of cars and bridges and tunnels and bells and whistles and the thought of all the noise made me shudder, but I tried to be nice about it because he meant it kindly. I hoped he wouldn't offer to reconstruct his space station for me.

I felt very sorry for myself. I thought it would have been much more fun to have had measles with everybody else, and if I'd had it then I wouldn't have been so sick; and Daddy wasn't home that evening and I wanted Daddy, and I resented Mother spending time with the others at bed time. It was really rather nice while everybody else was sick and I was taking care of Rob, but it was awful with me being sick all by myself and everybody else feeling fine.

I tried to go to sleep but I kept bouncing around and the sheets got all messed up again and I needed Suzy to fix them, and the aspirin didn't seem to have helped at all. The hall light was on and a shadow moved across it, and then John was standing in the doorway. "It's me again," he whispered. "Are you still awake?"

"How could I sleep when I feel so awful?" I asked. Maybe I was good when I was in the hospital after my bike accident, but I wasn't good about having measles.

"Mother wants to know if you want some more gingerale."

"I guess so."

He was back in a moment with a cool, amber glass, and I rose up on one elbow and sipped at it and began to feel a little better. The light coming in from the hall was just enough light not to hurt my eyes, and John was standing there by the bed looking sorry for me, and that helped, too. John has a way of making people feel that he cares what happens to them; that's one of the nicest things about him because it's true. He really does care.

"I've been out walking around the orchard," John said.

"It's late."

"Not that late. Just about eight thirty, and it isn't even quite dark around the edges. It'll be summer before we know it. The apple blossoms are just about to burst open. I'll pick you a bunch of violets tomorrow to put on your bookcase. I stood there and watched the stars come out. If you hadn't been measly I'd have come and got you, they were so beautiful."

"I've seen stars before," I said shortly.

"It's a funny thing about problems and being sick and everything," John said. "When you're in the middle of it, it seems so enormous, it seems the only thing in the world. But when you think of the relativity of size it doesn't seem to matter after all."

"Having measles matters to me even if it doesn't seem to matter to anyone else," I said, stuffily. "Anyhow, what do you mean by the relativity of size?"

John went to the east window and pushed aside the curtains. Our house is 100 miles

outside the city, so there are few lights to dim the stars. "Look at that star up there. Bright and beautiful but it's only a pinprick in the sky. If it has planets we can't see them. And then look at our own solar system."

"You look at it," I said, irritated.

John continued, undaunted. "We're on part of it right now. The earth. Just a small sphere, one of—how many planets is it? I forget."

We'd had it in school the year before, Mercury, Venus, Earth, Mars, Jupiter, Planetoids, Saturn, oh—what comes next, is it Pluto? I stuck my face in the pillow and mumbled, "I couldn't care less."

"Just one of maybe a dozen planets of assorted size circling about a larger ball that's our sun," John said. "And then think of the atoms that go to make everything up. That go to make *us* up."

"You think—" I started.

But John said quickly, "Shut up, Vicky, and listen. Do you realize that your body is made up of millions of atoms, and each one is a tiny solar system? And maybe some of these solar systems are like the larger one we live on. Maybe some of them have inhabited planets with flourishing civilizations. It's all a question of the relativity of size. We really don't know anything about size except that we don't understand it at all."

I shivered. I was hot with fever but I shivered anyhow. "Shut up. You make me feel as though I'm mostly thin air, when I think about being made out of atoms. And now to be made of inhabited planets—of all the idiotic notions, John Austin. What does that make me, a galaxy? Galaxy Austin, that's me."

"Well," John said, "Mother said I was just to give you the gingerale and see if I could help make you more comfortable for the night. She or Daddy'll look in on you later. Here, I'll straighten out your bed, you've got it all messed up." He pulled the bottom sheet from both sides till it was taut under me—my bed's an odd size that doesn't take fitted sheets—and turned over my pillow, and it felt better. Then he said good-night and left me, not a bit cross at me because of my bad temper, as I'd been at him the night he had grippe.

But that's what I mean about John. Things like that. Like talking to me about stars and the relativity of size and stuff. The other kids, the ones we go to school with, don't talk like that. It's not that John does it often, but he does it. It's partly, I suppose, because Mother and Daddy discuss things at table. And then Daddy belongs to a group of doctors that get together once a month to discuss things, not medicine, but philosophy and economics and stuff like that, and Daddy has been letting John sit and listen in when the meetings are at our house. But what I mean is, we're used to John. Until you get to really know John he can be difficult, but he's handsome and bright and infuriating and peculiar and our brother and we take him for granted.

But he isn't like anybody else's brother, and the other kids don't see him the way we do. One thing that has been a big help to him is having Dave Ulrich for a friend. Dave is a head shorter than John, but he's built like a bull; he's nearly two years older than John, but they're in the same grade, and it sort of makes John seem more okay to be seen with Dave. He and Dave don't discuss things; Dave's not a talker. They *do* things together. When they were little they started to dig a hole that would go all the way down to China.

18

They dug in Dave's back yard and they got down ten feet before Mr. Ulrich decided it was dangerous and ordered them to quit.

Then they built the tree house in our big maple, and they took a couple of old bikes and two old lawn mowers they bought for ten dollars and made a car that would run. Dave isn't very smart at school. I don't mean he's dumb or anything; his I.Q.'s probably fine. He just doesn't care about books unless he's looking something up about how to build one of his machines. This means he's okay in anything that's mathematical, but he'd probably flunk everything else if John didn't push him through. Dave's father has a big lumber business, and Dave's going to go in with him as soon as he gets out of high school, though I know Mrs. Ulrich wishes he'd study enough to go to college.

School work's always been easy for John. Lots of kids hide their report cards because they aren't very good, but John doesn't want people to see his because they're too good. He says it's bad enough being so near-sighted he can't see the blackboard without his glasses, so he's already pegged as being an egg head.

Suzy and I get good report cards, too, but not as good as John's. I'm good at English and spoken reports and history, but I have a terrible struggle with math. Suzy's memory will pull her through almost anything, and she says she has to get in the habit of getting reasonable report cards if she wants to get into medical school—and she does. Suzy and John have always known what they want to do when they're grown up; John wants to go into space in some way or other, and he's already reading a lot of astrophysics. And Suzy's wanted to be a doctor ever since she could talk. As for me—what? I wish I knew.

Mother and Daddy shake their heads about Rob; he has a big vocabulary; he plunges into words the way other people plunge into water, and no topic is too big or grown-up for him to discuss, from war to sex to pollution, but he's just learned to recognize the alphabet and he's not in the least interested in learning to read, and all the rest of us could read when we were five.

Maggy's report cards are up and down. She'd always been to private schools before she came to live with us, and she's ahead of her grade in some things, and behind in others. As to what she wants to do when she's grown up, she'd better marry a millionaire who can give her everything she wants.

But to get back to John. Of course the Sunday after I got measles I was still in bed, though I was beginning to feel lots better. I was still covered with rash and looked repulsive, but I did feel like playing a game of darts with John, and light didn't bother my eyes any more so I was working through a pile of books. I played and played Mother's records, and laughed at the funny ones and cried at the sad ones. And Saturday evening I got out of bed and went downstairs to watch a Cousteau TV special on endangered species.

Sunday morning, Mother made waffles for breakfast, and Suzy brought me up a tray with waffles and maple syrup and a cup of cocoa with a big blob of whipped cream on it, and it tasted marvelous, the first time anything had tasted really good since I started measles.

Then everybody started off for Sunday School and church and I curled up and took a little nap, and then pushed up my pillows and took a book from my pile and began to read. I was alone in the house but I had all the animals with me, so I wasn't lonely. Rochester lay on the floor by my bed, and Colette was on the foot of the bed, at my feet; Prunewhip, the splotchy colored cat, came patpatting upstairs and jumped on the bed, too, and sat on my chest and began purring loudly and then kneading her front claws into my neck. I kept shoving her paws away, or trying to push her claws back into their soft sheaths, but she was determined to enjoy herself in her own way, so I had to pull the blanket up over my neck and leave her to it.

I was deep in my book when I heard the kitchen door open and shut. I looked at my little clock that Grandfather gave me for Christmas, and it wasn't time for anybody to be home from church yet; I wondered who on earth it could be. Then I heard rather stealthy footsteps coming up the back stairs and I called out, "Who is it?"

Maggy's voice called back, "It's us," and I wondered what kind of trouble she'd got into now, and then she and John appeared in the doorway.

What a sight!

Maggy's black hair was wild, as though it hadn't been combed or brushed for several years, and her good Sunday dress was ripped, the skirt half pulled off the waist, and a big, jagged tear in one sleeve. And John! One of John's eyes was all swollen and puffy and there was a cut across his eyebrow and he didn't have on his glasses, and without his glasses John is half blind. His nose had been bleeding, too, and his collar was bloody and torn. It was obvious that Maggy had been crying, and I couldn't tell whether or not John had. I practically jumped out of bed, I was so startled. Colette started to bark, the high yelp she gives when she's upset. Prunewhip jumped down off the bed and swished out of the room. Rochester got up and went and stood by John and Maggy and growled, low and deep in his throat, as though to dare anybody to come near them when he was around.

John petted him, saying, "Oh, Rochester, I wish you'd been over in the churchyard half an hour ago."

"But what on earth happened?" I demanded.

John gave a very lopsided grin. "We were in a fight."

"Who? Why? Do Mother and Daddy know? Where are the others?"

"Hold it," John said. "We'd better go wash before we do anything else."

"No you don't!" I cried. "You tell me what happened first!"

John gave Maggy a funny kind of rough hug. John has never been one for hugging and kissing, and he and Maggy have never seen particularly eye to eye, anyhow, so this was all the more remarkable.

"I got involved in a monstrous battle," John said, "And Maggy was coming down from the Sunday School room and saw me, and she lit into the boys like a hurricane and did her best to rescue me. It was a doggone good best, too. If it hadn't been for Maggy I'd have had a sight worse licking than I got."

"But why were you getting a licking?" I asked. "Where was Dave?" I didn't think anybody'd dare pick a fight with John if Dave were around.

John gave that funny, lop-sided grin again and I realized that his lip was cut and swollen, too. "Dave has measles. Come on, Mag, let's wash up."

"No!" I shouted. "Tell me what happened."

"I think I'd better sit down," John said. "I feel wuzzy." He flopped into the rocker and closed his eyes, and his eyes without glasses were as strange-looking as the cuts and bruises on the rest of his face.

"Where are your glasses?" I asked.

"Smashed. You all right, Maggy?"

"No," Maggy said. "I'm mad. John was fighting all by himself with at least a dozen boys on top of him. It wasn't fair. And I didn't have a chance to run up to the Sunday School room to get Suzy or Rob to help. It wasn't fair. It was the meanest thing I ever saw."

"But what happened?" I asked again.

"Okay," John said, "Let's make it brief, Mag. Mr. Irving (he's the Sunday School superintendent) wasn't there. Nobody knew why he wasn't there. He came puffing up right after the big battle was over, and he'd had a flat tire coming up from Clovenford, but that was too late to do me any good."

"What does Mr. Irving have to do with it, anyhow?"

"Well, he always does the opening service for the Sunday School," John said, "you know that. Added to which, Mr. Vining's away this week."

Mr. Vining's the minister. And this explained nothing. "What's all this got to do with you?"

"When it was obvious Mr. Irving wasn't going to get to church on time, Mr. Ulrich asked me to do it," John said.

"To do what?"

John gave a funny sort of groan. "The opening service."

"It wasn't fair," Maggy protested again. "I heard Aunt Victoria telling Uncle Wallace Mr. Ulrich should never have asked it of John."

Mr. Ulrich teaches the high school Sunday School class, and I guess he's sort of second in charge if Mr. Irving isn't there, because sometimes he gives the opening service.

"But he asked me," John said. "He kind of looked around the church. He looked us all over, and his eye lit on me, and he said, 'I'm willing to bet John Austin can get up there and do the opening service for us. How about it, John?' What was I to do? There was nothing I wanted to do less, but I felt I was sort of stuck with it; if I didn't

24

do it I'd be letting Mr. Ulrich down—and Dave, too. At first I didn't say anything, and then Mr. Ulrich said, 'How about it, John?' and I said, 'Okay, Mr. Ulrich, I'll try.' And I had to get up and go to the front of the church and everybody was watching me and some of the boys were grinning, and I thought, I'll show them. So I gave the call to worship, and then had everybody sing *Holy, Holy, Holy*, to give myself time to think. Then I told one of Grandfather's stories, the one about the shoemaker who was so poor and yet he helped all those people—you know the one, it goes with the part in the Bible about if you do it unto the least of these you do it unto me."

"It was a wonderful story," Maggy said. "The girls all thought you were marvelous."

"Yes," John said, "that was the trouble. And I made one terrific goof."

"What?" I asked.

"I took off my glasses."

"But why! You know you can't see two feet in front of your nose without them."

"That's exactly why," John said. "I thought if I couldn't see the kids I wouldn't be so scared. I was afraid if somebody made a face at me or giggled or looked as though they thought I was a dope or something, I'd forget what I was saying and not be able to go through with it. So I took off my glasses so everybody'd look like a vague blur and I couldn't see who was who, or what they were thinking, or anything. But a lot of them thought I was doing it to show off."

"But you weren't—"

"Of course I wasn't. But they thought I was."

"It was those dopey girls," Maggy explained, "giggling and carrying on and saying how dreamy he looked without them."

"I don't think anybody listened to a word I said." John sighed, heavily. "That's almost the worst of it. Maybe some of the little kids listened to the story, but nobody else. Well, then we had the collection, and I had two of the smallest kids take it. Maybe that was being a coward, but I felt safer that way. And then I had to do the prayer."

"What did you say?" I asked. "Did you make it up?"

"No, I was too scared. I said the St. Francis Prayer." And he began to say it softly, as though he needed it for himself. "Lord, make me an instrument of your peace. Where there is hatred, let me sow love; where there is injury, pardon; where there is doubt, faith; where there is discord, union; where there is despair, hope; where there is darkness, light; and where there is sadness, joy. O divine master, grant that I may not so much seek to be consoled as to console; to be understood as to understand; to be loved as to love; for it is in giving that we receive; it is in pardoning that we are pardoned; and it is in dying that we are born to eternal life." He took a deep breath. "Well, then we went to our classes. But I knew trouble was coming. A couple of the kids kind of poked me and whispered things like, 'You just think you're the most beautiful boy, don't you?' And Mr. Ulrich made it worse by trying to set me up as an example to the rest of the class and I couldn't shut him up. If Dave had been there he'd have shut his father up. When classes were over the Sunday School teachers were supposed to be meeting about something, and the minute I got outdoors the kids were waiting for me, and one of them said, 'Got your glasses on now, haven't you, gorgeous?' and I said, 'Yeah, what's it to you,' and he said, 'Take 'em off so we can see those dreamy blue eyes,' and I said, 'Take 'em off yourself,' and that's how it started."

"They were cowards," Maggy said, "all of them together and John all alone, and when his glasses got busted they knew he couldn't even see what he was doing. But he was doing okay. I came out in the middle of it, 'cause someone told me what was going on, and I was just so mad I jumped on Sammy Heggie's back and pulled his hair and then I saw somebody else's leg sticking out and I bit that. I don't know whose it was, but I bet I drew blood."

"Kind of backhanded tactics," John said, "but they surely helped. The others weren't fighting exactly fair, either."

"What about Mother and Daddy?" I asked. "Do they know about it?"

"Dad brought us home," John said.

"Did he break it up?"

"No. One of the girls ran in and got the teachers out of their meeting and they all came out and everybody kind of got off me and Maggy was fighting so hard by then she didn't even realize the fight was over till Mr. Ulrich pulled her off one of the boys. Then people started coming to church, and Mother and Daddy came up the path and saw us, and Dad brought us home, and that's all."

Maggy gave a contented sort of sigh. "Maybe Suzy and Rob don't even know about it yet. They were in the upstairs Sunday School room."

"Somebody's told them by now," I said.

John stood up. "Well, I guess I better grope my way to the bathtub. I'll take the upstairs bathroom, it's colder, and you can use the one downstairs, Mag."

Maggy ran off, and I thought she seemed different than she had been with us. Mostly she's pulled against us, tried to be different, to have special privileges, to be a TV star, and suddenly she seemed not only more like one of us, but as though she actually finally wanted to be one of us.

John said, "Well, see you later, Vic," and went off with Rochester thumping anxiously at his heels. I heard him bump into a chair or something, and then a moment later I heard his bathwater running. I lay in bed, stroking Colette's ear, and thinking about what had happened, till John came back in, wrapped in his bath towel, and sat down in the Boston rocker again.

"I get on okay with Dave," he said. "I thought I got on okay with the others, too."

I wasn't sure what to say. I murmured, "Oh, John . . ." and if I'd been Mother I could have gone to him and put my arms around him and given him some love. But I was only his kid sister, Vicky, and all I could do was lie there and look at him, his body firm and lean and still white from winter, his face all battered up, and the cut by his eye going right through one of his eyebrows. Without his glasses his eyes seemed much bigger than usual, and they looked unhappy. His reddy-brown hair was wet, and he'd slicked it down, but a tuft of it stuck up in the back.

"Well," I said at last, "Maybe it comes down to muffins again." (About muffins I will explain in just a minute.)

John nodded. "Sometimes being muffiny can be very tempting. Listen, Vicky, as soon as you're better let's have a meeting. Is it okay if I propose Maggy? As far as I'm concerned, she qualified this morning."

I remembered Maggy's look as she'd gone down the hall to take her bath, so I said, "It's okay with me if you think it'll be okay with the others."

"We've never turned down anybody anyone's put up, yet."

"It's never been anybody who didn't belong here," I said, "and Maggy's really only a visitor."

"That's a muffiny remark if there ever was one," John said.

I thought it over for a moment. "Yes, I guess it was."

"Do I look awful?" he asked.

"Kind of like a prize fighter."

"That's one thing I'm not and never will be. Well, I'd better go get some clothes on."

He'd just gone out the door when the phone rang, and he headed into Mother and Daddy's room, bumping into things on the way.

I heard him say, "Dave! . . . But you have measles! . . . Well, it wasn't your father's fault. . . . No, if I'd done it differently, or something . . . well, sure I'm not mad at him. . . . They home from church already? . . . Well, sure, I'm mad at the others. I was so mad by the time they broke it up I was beginning to enjoy the fight. . . . Listen, you'd better get back to bed. You don't want any secondary infections. . . . Sure. Be over to see you as soon as you're feeling better. Hey, Dave, I sure look a beaut, you ought to see me. . . . Okay. Bye."

As he hung up I heard the door downstairs open, and Colette leaped off my bed and dashed down, barking her welcoming bark; and then there was the sound of a small herd of elephants and Suzy and Rob came dashing up the stairs. And then Mother and Daddy came along and then the telephone rang again, and it was the father of one of the kids in the fight, to complain

30

about John's starting it! And the rest of the day was like that, a peaceful Sunday, all full of sound and fury.

Mr. Ulrich called, very upset, and Mother had to reassure him that John wasn't seriously hurt, and he really wasn't to blame, it was just one of those things. The father of another of the boys called up in a rage because John had given his boy a bloody nose, and Daddy told him off about that.

In between times Daddy cleaned up John's face and put a bandage over the cut above his eye, and told him not to read till his glasses were fixed. Maggy had a big scratch on one leg, but otherwise it was her clothes that got it; she was okay. And Mr. Irving, the Sunday School superintendent, called up, all worried, and Daddy had to calm him down. "Look, boys will be boys and problems like this happen occasionally. Nobody was badly hurt, and maybe they've all learned a lesson. But let's not have the whole village get into a turmoil over it." All in all we had about as much Sunday peace and quiet as we'd have had at a three ring circus.

The next day one of the Granby boys got into real trouble. He 'borrowed' one of the Hendricks' horses and the horse stepped into a hole and sprained its foot, and he was scared to tell the Hendricks he'd taken the horse and what had happened, but of course he didn't get away with it, and in the ensuing excitement John and the Sunday School fight got forgotten. John got new glasses and his face unswelled and his cuts healed and things went back to normal.

A week later I went back to school, and so did Dave, and suddenly we were plunged into summer. It had been a long, cold, snowy, rainy spring. In fact, that was hardly any real spring to speak of at all, and then all at once at the end of May it was summer, with hot, sunny days and swimming in the pond after school, and we all went to sleep lying on top of our beds with the covers pulled down, and Mother and Daddy pulled our sheets up when they came upstairs at night.

That Friday at breakfast John asked if we could have a picnic up Hawk Mountain that night.

"Why, John? I don't see why not, but is it for anything special?"

"Yes," he said. "Muffins. We want to take in a new member."

"I see. Okay with the others?"

"The picnic or the member?"

"Both."

"The picnic's fine. I haven't brought the member up yet."

Maggy was putting her cereal dish in the sink, something it took her months to remember to do. Mother glanced at her. "Am I right in my guess as to the new member?"

John grinned. "Could be."

"All right, John. Just don't make it too late for the little ones, will you? What do you want to take for supper?"

"Can Dave and I build a fire?"

Mother considered. "You're both scouts and I trust you, but I'd really rather you didn't if there aren't going to be any adults there, because of the little ones."

"Okay, then, could you make us a big dish of baked beans with hot dogs cut up in it? You know the kind. If we start out with it good and hot it'll be okay. I thought I'd ask Dave and Betsey to bring a salad, and Izzy and Nannie Irving can bring ice cream and coke."

"All right," Mother said. "I'll drive you up at five and come for you at nine. Okay?"

"Thanks," John said. "That'll be super."

So at five we got in the car, the four of us and Maggy, and picked up Dave and Betsey, and Izzy and Nannie, and Pedro Xifra. John didn't ask Pedro to bring anything, because his parents don't have much money and aren't likely to. Mr. Xifra's a tenant farmer, and he stays on Creighton's farm and works long hard hours with little time for his family. Pedro helps out as much as he can when he gets home from school and weekends. We knew he'd worked extra hard to be ready when we came for him.

First we stopped off for Dave and Betsey. Dave had a big wooden bowl with tomatoes and celery and Betsey a tea towel wrapped around lettuce and a big jar of dressing to pour over it. Luckily at the last minute Mother'd remembered we'd need something to eat our food with, and off, so we had a stack of paper plates and cups and forks as well as our hot dish of beans. I think Mr. Ulrich still feels kind of bad about John, because just as we were about to leave he came up from his lumber yard in Clovenford and handed

us a big box of cookies. Then we went to get the
Irvings. They live in a white house with black
shutters on the main street right next to their
store. There are Izzy and Nannie, and then there
are the boys, one and two years old! Izzy and
Nannie take a lot of the care of their baby
brothers so Mrs. Irving can help in the store. As
well as being the store keeper and the Sunday
School superintendent, Mr. Irving plays the
'cello with a string quartet in Clovenford. In the
summer they often give concerts and a lot of the
summer people go to hear them. Izzy plays the
piano and is learning the organ, and Nannie can't
tell one note from the other. Mr. Irving put a big
case of soda in the back of our station wagon, and
Izzy and Nanny had ice cream packed in dry ice.

Then we went to get Pedro. He's in the middle of a whole lot of kids. Their house is across the road from the barns, and needs painting, and last summer their stoop started to fall off, and it would have fallen off if Pedro hadn't fixed it.

He was waiting for us by the mail box. He had a brown paper bag with him and he said he'd made egg salad sandwiches. John said, "Oh, swell, Pedro," and I could see he felt kind of bad about it, though the eggs must have come from Pedro's own chickens.

Mother drove the station wagon, which was by now pretty jammed, up the dirt road to the top of Hawk, and we all tumbled out, carrying the picnic stuff. Mother waved and honked and took off, and John and Izzy got the picnic all organized, and we ate and talked and laughed and the evening was warm, but not hot, with a breeze cool enough so that we put on our sweaters or jackets.

When we'd cleaned everything up, and put all the trash in the big trash can, John said, "You've probably all guessed what we're here for."

"It looks like a meeting of the anti-muffin club," Pedro said.

"How'd you guess? And I wanted a meeting because I'm proposing a new member."

He was smiling, and I looked over at Maggy and she was sitting looking a little pink and flustered.

Pedro said, "If it's Maggy, I'm all for it," and smiled at her.

Nannie said, "It must be Maggy, because all the rest of us are members."

John said to Pedro, "We had a whopperoozo of a fight in the churchyard, and Maggy pitched in to help me, and didn't give a hoot what anybody thought."

Pedro wasn't around at the fight, because his family goes to St. Francis' church in Clovenford.

Izzy asked, "Does she know about muffins? Do you, Maggy?"

Maggy said, "I like them when Aunt Victoria makes them for breakfast," and everybody laughed, even Rob. One thing Rob's learned is that he couldn't belong, being so much younger than the rest of us, if he made any noise or disturbance, and he was so thrilled at being included in something that had so many big kids in it, that he sat quiet as a little mouse at all the meetings, with an expression so solemn it was funny. The main reason we let Rob be in the club was that it was a family thing, and then got expanded, and if ever anybody was perfect anti-muffin material, it's Rob. Added to which, he really kind of started the club.

"We'd better tell her about muffins, then," Nannie said. "That is, if she's really interested."

"I'm not exactly hungry right now," Maggy patted her stomach, "but I'm fascinated." Her black hair was pushed back from her ears and it fell softly down to her shoulders. Her face looked white against it and her eyes were dark. Even though she had on jeans and an old red sweater that had once been mine, I thought that in comparison with the rest of us she looked very much a city person.

There was a pause while everybody waited for somebody else to speak. Betsey said, "John or one of the Austins ought to tell her about it, because they started it."

"Well," John said, "Rob really started it. It was about a year ago, and Uncle Douglas was up for the week-end."

Uncle Douglas is Daddy's brother, ten years younger than Daddy, and a painter, and we all love him.

John continued, "He came up without a girl, but the week-end before he came up *with* a girl."

"Does he always bring his girls up?" Maggy asked.

"Usually. We kind of look them over. Some of them we like and some of them we don't like and we didn't like this one."

"Sort of like Sally?" Maggy asked.

"Even worse, and younger. She kept asking questions about the family, Mother's and Daddy's families," I said, "wanting to know all about forebears and stuff."

John started laughing. "Remember the aunt's sisters?"

I laughed, too. It was really hilarious. This girl kept talking about her ancestors, and Rob went to Mother and said, "Her aunt must have had an awful lot of sisters."

So John told about that and we all laughed, the way you laugh an extra lot on a picnic when you've filled up with good food and are feeling warm and happy.

Maggy said, "I still don't know about muffins."

So John explained. What happened was that Uncle Douglas came back the next week-end and told us that he and the girl were through. And then he gave us a sort of lecture, about how we shouldn't worry about families and the right ethnic background (I looked at Pedro as John was explaining), but you should like them or dislike them for themselves. And Uncle Douglas went on to say that his ex-girl thought that where people were born made them what they are.

38

Well, that same afternoon, about a year ago, Prunewhip had kittens. We knew she was going to have kittens, and we ran down to the cellar to her bed, but she wasn't there, and we looked in the garage and Daddy's office and under all the beds and in the closets and everywhere we could think of, but we couldn't find her. Then, when Mother went to turn on the oven for the muffins she was making, she noticed that the oven door was part way open, and she opened it all the way, and there was Prunewhip with five kittens! We'd had kittens all over the place, but never in the oven before, and Prunewhip looked very pleased with herself, and Mother said, ah, well, we'd do without the oven that evening.

And John said, a bit sarcastically, "Uncle Douglas, would your ex-girl think the kittens were muffins because they were born in the oven?" Rob thought that was awfully funny and when he stopped laughing he started chanting.

"Kittens are muffins
In ovens and puffins,"

Suzy interrupted and said, "They'd all have to be exactly alike, each one just like the other, instead of all different like Prunewhip's kittens."

John said, suddenly serious, "I'd hate that. But that's what a lot of people want—everybody the same like a row of muffins."

So that's how the muffin club got started. Maggy thought it was rather funny and said, "Go on, tell me more."

"Well, that's really it," John said. "You can see how we went on from the kittens not being muffins because they were born in the oven, to

starting the anti-muffin club. Uncle Douglas says it will help us avoid the dangers of conformity."

Izzy lay on her back, looking up at the deepening sky. "Your Uncle Douglas is very nice, but most of the time I don't know what he's talking about."

"All he means is that you shouldn't be afraid to be yourself, even if it means being different."

"Like lots of grown ups," Betsey said. "Most of them. Always so worried about what somebody's going to think."

"So do you want to belong?" Suzy asked.

Funnily enough, Maggy got all flustered. "I'd love to, if you really want me."

"We wouldn't have called the meeting if we didn't," Suzy said. "We thought maybe you'd think it was silly."

"Why?" Maggy sounded indignant.

Nannie said, "Just that it's something you've probably never had to think about before, with the way you lived before you came to stay with the Austins."

Maggy asked stiffly, "What do you mean?"

John said quickly, "Well, you've never been much around muffiny people. Your grandfather's certainly not a muffin. And your parents don't sound as though they were much like most people, your father being a test pilot, for instance. And Aunt Elena's certainly not a muffin.

She goes around giving concerts and practices at least five hours a day and it certainly doesn't bother her that she isn't like anybody else."

"Is Uncle Douglas an anti-muffin?" Maggy asked.

"Well, sure."

"And Aunt Victoria and Uncle Wallace? Do they belong to the club?"

"They're certainly anti-muffins," I said, "but they don't belong to the club."

"Why not?"

"If you start putting parents in it can get complicated," John said. "Sometimes there are parents who are muffins and children who aren't, and vice versa." Nobody said anything. It was a little ticklish. We're terribly fond of the Ulrichs, but they're really kind of muffiny. Mr. Irving certainly isn't a muffin, practicing his 'cello in the back room of the store when there aren't many customers; but Mrs. Irving is; she's always worrying about what the neighbors will think, and since they run the store and are always in the public eye, the neighbors know a good deal about them. The Xifra's aren't muffins, but then, on the other hand, they aren't anti-muffins either, except Pedro, and I think Mrs. Xifra'd really love to be a muffin.

"Could I ask another question?" Maggy asked.

"Sure."

"What's the point to this club?"

"There isn't any particular point," John said. "Just to help us not act like muffins, I guess. If you know there are other people who feel the same way you do, then it gives you courage to stand up for your principles. You were acting anti-muffiny when you ploughed into all those kids after Sunday School. You weren't worried about what they were going to think of you, or if you were going to be hurt, or if it was going to make you unpopular."

"Oh," Maggy said. "Like that new girl who came into our grade last week. "She comes from Tennessee and she has a funny accent and everybody teases her. You mean if I go up to her on Monday and try to be nice to her, and see what she's really like, and don't care what the others think of me for doing it, that'll be anti-muffin."

"Good," Pedro approved. "That's it, Maggy. I used to have an accent, too, when I started school. John and Dave kept my life from being hell."

"And it's partly just for fun," John said, "the club, I mean. We don't have any officers or dues or special times for meetings or anything. It's just a time people who like each other can get together and have a good time, the way we're doing this evening."

"Let's sing," Izzy suggested. "Nannie'll sing us a solo."

Nannie was lying on her back chewing a fresh new blade of grass. "I might surprise you some day," she said lazily.

Izzy started singing the Ash Grove. We all love the Welsh melody, and we sing it to words

Mr. Irving taught us, and it's kind of the anti-muffin song.

"His law he enforces,
the stars in their courses,
the sun in his orbit
obediently shine."

Izzy sang, and we all joined in.

"The hills and the mountains,
The rivers and fountains,
The deeps of the ocean
Proclaim God Divine.

We too should be voicing
Our love and rejoicing
With glad adoration
A song let us raise,

Till all things now living
Unite in thanksgiving,
To God in the highest,
Hosanna and praise!"

Izzy's clear, pure soprano was like a flute. Rob got up from where he was sitting and plunked himself down in front of Izzy and put his head in her lap. Izzy started ruffling his soft, light brown hair, and kept on singing, and Rob closed his eyes and I knew that in a few minutes he would be asleep. Then Izzy started the Tallis Canon. We all know the parts to that, so we joined in. John was singing bass, and I suddenly realized how deep his voice was, and it seemed hardly any time since it had been high and clear like Rob's. Izzy was looking at him, and her eyes were like Colette's when she looks at Daddy when he's sitting in the red leather chair and she hopes he's going to give her a tid-bit. And suddenly I

44

realized that John was growing up, and Izzy and Betsey were beginning to wear make-up as a matter of course. We were all growing up and everything was going to change; it would never be the same again. I felt absolutely desolate with sadness, and suddenly I jumped up, shouting, "Let's play something silly, let's play Touch Tag," and the next minute we were all running around wildly, and John and Izzy and Pedro and Dave just as laughing and panting as the rest of us, and I felt a little better. We ran and shouted till it got dark, and then we sat down again and watched the stars come out and Pedro told us about them, the names of the different constellations, and how far away the stars are, and how big.

"We were going with Mother and Daddy to study the stars, the night—" Suzy stopped herself, and I knew she had been going to say, "the night Uncle Hal was killed, and Maggy's father had been Uncle Hal's co-pilot."

"What night?" Maggy asked.

We hadn't gone, and the autumn had slipped away and winter had come and we hadn't gone.

"What night?" Maggy asked again.

"One night last autumn," John said, "before you came. Is that Vega of the Lyre, Pedro?"

Pedro pointed out Vega for John, and then he said, "I love stars. I'm going to learn everything I can about them. I love them better than anything in the world. Better even than people or books. I'd give my right arm to work at Palomar or Mount Wilson or some place like that."

"Maybe you will," I said. I like Pedro a lot. When he decides he wants to learn something, or change in some way, he usually manages to do it.

"Well, I'm going to Regional Trade School," Pedro said, "to learn to be the electrician I've always wanted to be, but stars will be my lifelong hobby. Hey, look, kids, a shooting star! You don't see many in May."

"The thing about stars," Pedro went on, "is that when you're with stars, people don't matter so much, or things like being dirty and untidy and

quarreling, and nobody else caring about anything you care about, and things like that."

"We care," Nannie said softly.

And John tried to lighten things by giving me a poke and saying, "It's all a question of the relativity of size."

"I hear a car," Suzy said. "I bet it's Mother."

It was, but she didn't rush us home. Instead, she came and sat with us for a few minutes first, so we didn't have any feeling of being pushed when we finally piled into the station wagon. Rob

was so sound asleep that we had to carry him, and he slept in my lap all the way home, and then Daddy came out and carried him up to bed. So of course he was asleep when we said prayers and didn't hear when Maggy said in her God Bless, "And thank you, God, for the best time I ever had."